In *The Reboot*, Stephen Hiemstra masterfully weaves a story that is both imaginative and deeply grounded in timeless truths. With characters that wrestle with faith, identity, and purpose, Hiemstra invites readers into a world where the struggles of youth and the echoes of history collide in surprising ways. This is a compelling read that lingers in the heart long after the last page.

Eric Teitelman
House of David Ministries

I recommend Stephen's book most heartily. He is a most learned man who writes with skills that make his books understandable and valuable. He can surprise the reader with the unexpected. Then, he can come to a conclusion that is gratifying to the reader. He is a gifted communicator!

Percy M. Burns
Author of Glorious Freedom

The Reboot, a sequel to *Jeez and the Gentile*, transports college student Tom back to the times of Jesus, where together with Jeez Tom travels along bandit-ravaged trails in Israel and then takes a highly risky sea journey to Rome, all the while embroiled in the dangerous politics of the Roman empire.

This is a multi-dimensional story, revealing both adventurous life in the world of Christ 2000 years ago, and at the same time the character development of Tom and Jesus himself. It's a great read for any young adult curious about life in the age of Jesus, and how this all relates to life today.

Brien Benson
Fairfax Collegiate

What a thrill to adventure again with the Fearsome Threesome. For those new to Scripture, biblical truths unfold with surprising clarity at the nexus of modern language and ancient context. For more seasoned scripture readers, familiar voices and scenes reemerge, intricately woven into a narrative tapestry of carefully researched practices and places.

Alexis Anderson
Communications strategist, Bible scholar,
and mom of 3 teens.

In Stephen Hiemstra's split-time novel, *The Reboot*, the sword of Tiberius, Poseidon's storm, Pan's Gates of Hell, and the intrigues of the Judeo-Roman world are interwoven in Jeez and Tom's search for the callings on their lives. Tom discovers his calling as he returns to his time. Jeez answers the call of a broken world.

Sharron Giambanco

The author again takes Tom on an adventurous journey back in time. The college-aged Tom returns again to Nazareth and collaborates with Jeez and Mary Magdalene. The three travel as Roman auxiliaries from Caesarea to Rome, combating danger along the way and meeting historical characters from Biblical times. Amid their service as Roman guards, both Tom and Jeez face the dilemmas regarding their future callings. If you enjoy time travel, adventure and the history and culture of the first century Roman Empire, this book is for you.

Claudette Renalds

Author of four novels including Rescuing Grace

This novella focuses on a theme we struggle with today more than ever—identity, especially our identity in Jesus Christ. In this book we can follow the trials of a young college student, Tom, who—like us—has too easily strayed from his calling, but with Jesus' help finds his way back. This book is perfect for anyone who has wondered what to do when the path forward is less than obvious.

Sofía Martínez Lafarga

Video Blogger[1]

---

1 https://www.youtube.com/@sofiaisabellapiano/featured

Other Books by the Author

Image of God Series
Image of God in the Parables[2]
Image of the Holy Spirit and the Church[2]
Image of God in the Person of Jesus

Christian Spirituality Series
A Christian Guide to Spirituality[1]
Life in Tension[2]
Called Along the Way
Simple Faith
Living in Christ
Image and Illumination

Masquerade Series[3]
Masquerade
The Detour
Christmas in Havana

Jeez and the Gentile Series[3]
Jeez and the Gentiles
The Reboot

Prayerbooks
Everyday Prayers for Everyday People
Prayers[2]
Prayers of a Life in Tension

[1] Also available in Spanish and German.
[2] Also available in Spanish.
[3] These books have been adapted as screenplays.

THE REBOOT

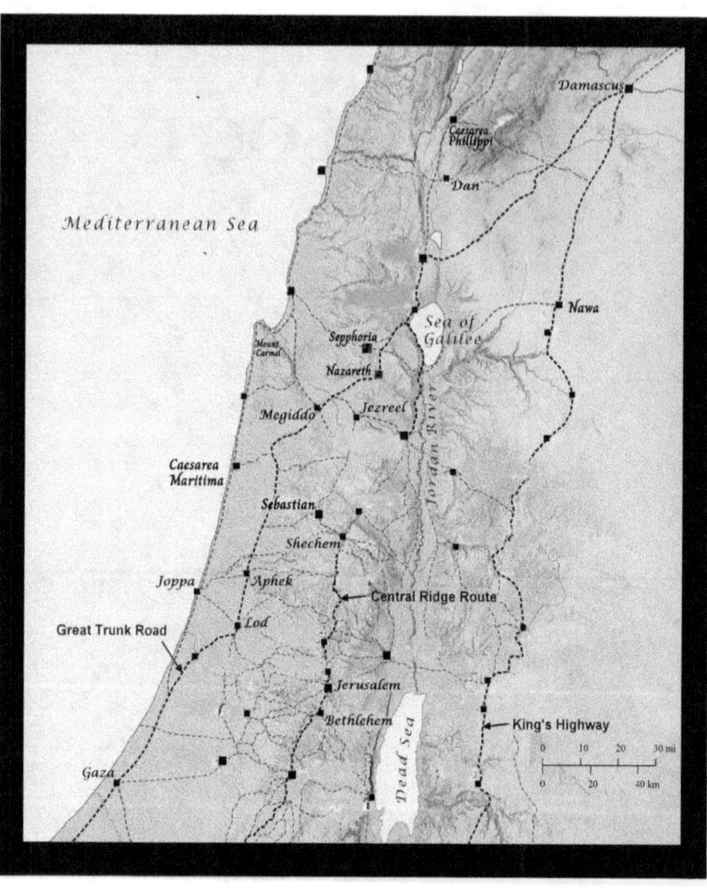

Map of Ancient Israel

THE REBOOT

Stephen W. Hiemstra

T2PNEUMA PUBLISHERS LLC
CENTREVILLE, VIRGINIA

The Reboot

This book is a work of fiction. Names, characters, places, and incidents are the product of the author's imagination or are used fictitiously. Any resemblance to actual events, locales, or persons, living or dead is coincidental.

T2Pneuma Publishers LLC
P.O. Box 230564, Centreville, Virginia 20120
www.T2Pneuma.com

Names: Hiemstra, Stephen W., 1953-, author. Title: The Reboot / Stephen W. Hiemstra. Series: Jeez and the Gentile Description: Centreville, VA: T2Pneuma Publishers LLC, 2025. Identifiers: LCCN: 2025918740 | ISBN: 978-1-942199-64-9 (paperback) | 978-1-942199-91-5 (KDP) | 978-1-942199-55-7 (epub) Subjects: LCSH Jesus Christ--Fiction. | Time travel--Fiction. | Israel--History--Fiction. | Rome--History--Tiberius, 42 B.C.-39 A.D.--Fiction | Coming of age--Fiction. | Christian fiction. | BISAC YOUNG ADULT FICTION / Religious / Christian / General | YOUNG ADULT FICTION / Religious / Christian / Historical | YOUNG ADULT FICTION / Religious / Christian / Action & Adventure Classification: LCC PS3608.I46 R43 2025 | DDC 813.6--dc23

Many thanks to my editors Jean Arnold, Claudette Renalds, and Harim Sanchez. I would also like to recognize comments by Paul Lauerman.

The cover art is called *The Grotto of Pan* by C. Hiemstra. Used with permission.

ACT ONE

Chapter One

*A*t eleven o'clock on a chilly Thursday evening, May 12th, an eighteen-year-old freshman, Thomas Timmerman, who goes by Tom, studied in his dorm room in Cambridge, Massachusetts. Late as it was, Tom sat at his desk, looking like a preppie Marine with his crew-cut light-brown hair, blue button-down shirt and striped tie, and khaki pants. Resting with its head on Tom's lap, is a golden retriever, Climate.

Tom's cell phone buzzed, Climate jumps, and he noticed a text from his perky, big-eyed girlfriend, Micha, who bristled at the mention of her American-ized name and still lived in warmer McLean, Virginia, waitressed at her parent's Korean-American restau-rant, and attended the community college. Tom picked up his phone.

Micha: What's up?

Micha sat on a couch dressed in an oversized pink Sailor Moon T-shirt and white shorts. Her long black hair, perfectly combed, flowed down her back. Athletic, thin-boned, and wearing no make-up, she debated to herself whether or not her preppie Marine had hung up his blue blazer yet.

Tom: *I'm studying biology.*

Micha smiled. The blue blazer was clearly hung up.

Micha: *Biology? What's with biology? I thought you studied criminal justice.*

Tom: *I'm pre-med now.*

Micha scratched her head.

Micha: *What happened to following your dad's footsteps and the police officer plan?*

Tom: *My grandparents pushed me to consider medicine.*

Micha looked worried, remembering how Tom's grandparents always flaunted their wealth at her expense.

Micha: *How's that going?*

Tom: *I'm acing the exams and being inundated with pre-med pinups wanting to be my lab partner.*

Previously slouching, Micha straightened up.

Micha: *So, you're surrounded by sirens. Have you found someone new?*

Tom: *No. I got called into the dean's office for grossing out several lab partners.*

Micha snapped her head.

Micha: *Grossing out lab partners? So, not sirens, but harpies?*

Tom: *Three former female lab partners complained to the dean about my presumed spearing of cat eyeballs and snapping of ligaments at them in the dissecting lab. They even showed him a deepfake video of an incident.*

Micha pursed her lips.

Micha: *What's that about?*

Tom: *You don't want to know.*

Micha paused, pulled her hair horizontally in distress with both hands.

Micha: *Sunday is Pentecost. Is your youth group planning anything?*

Tom: *No idea.*

Micha fidgeted.

Micha: *Have you dropped youth group?*

Tom: *I have been busy.*

Micha tried to empathize.

Micha: *That doesn't sound like you.*

Tom: *Got to go.*
Micha teared up.

Micha: *Later.*

Tom put his phone down and went back to reading his biology assignment in front of a photograph of him and Micha posing at the lion exhibit at the zoo. Tired and unable to concentrate, he put on his jogging outfit, snapped a leash on Climate, and went out to run. Returning at midnight reinvigorated like a monk after praying matins, he took a shower, read for two more hours, turned off the desk lamp, and slipped into bed.

∞

An eighteen-year-old Jeez changed into his robe in the Sepphoris barracks by the light of a breakfast fire just before dawn on Friday morning AD 15 in preparing to celebrate *Shavuot Shabbath* in Nazareth. His seven roommates snapped to attention. Jeez turned to spy Centurion Marcellus, and he straightened up like the others.

"I have bad news," Marcellus said, as the fireplace crackled in the background, and the smoke filled the room. "Your weekend furlough will have to wait."

"Sir?" Jeez replied.

"King Antipas requests your immediate presence at the palace. Change into your uniform and follow me."

"Yes, Sir," Jeez disrobed, dropped his robe in his chest, and put on his uniform. Marcellus turned, and the two exited at double-pace.

∞

On Friday morning, Tom breakfasted quickly in the dorm cafeteria dressed in cargo shorts, a black college T-shirt, and brown leather walking shoes. After finishing half a toasted bagel, he returned briefly to his room, brushed his teeth, and put on a baseball cap. Then he hiked over to the bookstore on the square to check out the textbooks in the stacks for summer classes in biochemistry and the calculus sequence. There he ran into a former lab partner, wearing a flashy white summer-print dress with red polka dots.

"Hey, don't you feel guilty for being such a

weirdo?" Cynthia said slyly, turning away from him to show off her long, bright-red hair and stunning figure, while looking over her shoulder.

"Should I?" Tom responded.

"How did your talk with the dean go?" Cynthia said. She turned again to give him a look out of the side of her eye.

"We're besties. You know. The dean and I got a real laugh out of the deepfake video of the alleged incident."

"Really? That's so interesting," Cynthia went on. "Do you have plans tonight? South Hall is hosting a kegger."

"You live in South Hall? Isn't South Hall a sorority catering to silver-spooners?" Tom asked.

"So, you have heard of us?" Cynthia asked rhetorically.

"Is it my imagination, or were all my previous lab partners friends of yours?"

Cynthia smiled. "Well, if you get bored studying, come over after eight."

"Sure thing," Tom said, matter-of-factly.

Cynthia walked off, pretending to look at other books.

∞

Tom hurried to a meeting with his chemistry tutor, who quizzed him on the periodic table. Tom's photographic memory made the whole session seem pointless. Following an hour of endless prodding, the tutor stopped and asked to borrow Tom's composition book.

"Academics don't seem to challenge you much. Call the coordinator at this hospital," The tutor wrote a telephone number in Tom's composition book. "Go volunteer at the hospital. Perhaps, working with doctors and patients will provide the challenge that you need," The tutor handed Tom the notebook and looked at him earnestly.

"Sure thing," Tom said. "Any other advice?"

"Don't lose focus," The tutor advised. "Lost opportunities are a theme today. Many talented students never realize their potential because of the many distractions of youth."

"Distractions of youth? Hmm. Sounds familiar," Tom observed.

∞

Tom left his tutor's office and walked over to the dorm cafeteria where he met his suitemates, who performed in a local vaudeville act. Dressed in cheap suits with collared grey, brown, and black shirts buttoned at the top. Everyone called them Larry, Moe, and Curley. The suitemates all picked up trays, went through the line, and lunch together at a table.

"What have you guys been up to?" Tom asked.

"This is open house week at the school-sanctioned clubs," Curley responded. "I visited the French Club that recruits students interested in cooking."

"You mean eating," Moe retorted.

"Ha, ha," Curley shot back. "The rumor is that the French Club is ninety-nine percent female."

"You guys are no fun," Larry chimed in. "I auditioned for the Music Club. Members play in the marching band and get free admission to games."

"But you don't play an instrument," Curley observed.

"They are also looking for cheerleaders with a lot of spirit," Larry said.

"What about you, Moe? Did you visit an open house?" Tom asked.

"I toured the Tower Club," Moe said.

"You mean the guys bungee jumping and sky-diving?" Larry observed. "Are you a super thrill-seeker?"

"Really?" Tom inquired.

"Actually, the club has a lot of hot gymnasts who tour with summer circus groups," Moe grinned.

"Tom, aren't you going to check out a club?" Larry asked.

"Sorry. I forgot about the whole club thing," Tom responded. "What do you know about the kegger this evening at South Hall?"

"Nada. The rumor going around is that South-Hall-kegger invites are a siren pickup line. Do you by any chance have a hot date tonight?" Larry asked.

"That fits," Tom noted.

∞

Jeez followed Marcellus to King Antipas' palace, a short distance from the barracks, where they found Tribune Claudius waiting out front.

Marcellus and Jeez saluted. "Marcellus and Jeez reporting as ordered."

Claudius stroked his beard. "Hmm. Follow me," He instructed, walking them into the palace throne room, where they found Antipas seated, surrounded by his attendants. Claudius stopped and removed his helmet. Marcellus and Jeez followed suit. Antipas motioned for Claudius to approach his throne.

"Is this the auxiliary that you spoke of?" Antipas nodded towards Jeez.

"Yes. This is Jeez," Claudius responded.

Antipas motioned for Jeez to approach the throne. Jeez stepped forward.

"Claudius tells me that you're trustworthy and reliable," Antipas announced.

"Thank you, your majesty," Jeez responded.

Antipas continued. "My brother, Philip, just returned from a trip to Rome, where he visited with our brother, Herod, and his wife, Herodias. Ride to Caesarea Philippi, inquire about Philip's health, and bring back word from our brother in Rome."

"Yes, sir," Jeez responded.

Antipas wrote these instructions on parchment, rolled them up, and sealed them. "Give this letter to Philip," Antipas handed him the parchment.

"Very good," Jeez responded.

Antipas continued. "The road to Caesarea Philippi is plagued with brigands. Pick one or more companions from your ranks to accompany you."

Antipas dismissed Marcellus and Jeez, but asked Claudius to remain. Marcellus and Jeez backed out of the throne room, turned, put on their helmets, and left the palace.

As they left the palace, a young man in a tattered robe feigned the use of a crutch, approached Marcellus to ask for alms. After Marcellus waived him off, the young man followed Marcellus and Jeez within earshot like a puppy at their heels, listening to their conversation.

Walking back to the barracks, Marcellus said. "Pick your companions carefully. The last courier to Caesarea Philippi was found stripped naked and hanging from a tree."

Jeez cringed.

"Now, ride to Nazareth and celebrate *Shavuot Shabbath* with your family for a few hours before you leave."

After Jeez disappeared into the barracks, the young spy reported his findings to Dante, a centurion of the Sebastian cohort, who wears a hooded robe over his uniform.

Chapter Two

*A*fter a run and an early dinner Tom returned to his room, pulled down the window shades, and lay on his bed for a brief nap. A white-noise recording of beach sounds played on his laptop.

Larry stopped by the suite to pick up his books on his way to class. "Catching a wink before your hot date tonight?"

"Nah. I just overdid a run earlier."

"Later."

Staring at the ceiling above, he day-dreamed about Cynthia, closed his eyes and fell asleep.

∞

Tom woke Friday afternoon leaning against a stone pine along a walkway down the hill from Sepphoris. The flapping of wings alerted him to a pair of turtle doves that came to rest on a branch in the tree above. When he opened his eyes, a gentle breeze blanketed his entire body with dry heat.

Before Tom has regained his wits, he noticed an eighteen-year-old Jeez stood in front of him wearing an auxiliary's uniform and holding the reins of three horses behind him, one loaded with supplies.

"Welcome back," Jeez said as if it had only been a couple hours since they last spoke. He still looked thin, but the auxiliary's uniform no longer wrapped around him as previously.

Tom realized that he too was uniformed, dressed as departed six-years prior. "You are a sight for sore eyes. Was it something that I said or did to earn this honor?" Tom inquired.

"No. Election is a not earned. You and I work well together, and I need your help," Jeez said.

"Help? My help?" Tom answered, looking puzzled. "I don't remember being much help when we got together six years ago."

"Remember? Don't you remember? After Damien and his crew killed my father, Joseph, you discovered his diversion, disclosed his deceit, and dismembered his duplicity."

"I remember Leo played an upscale role in all that, and it was Claudius that lifted Damien's head," Tom said.

"Perhaps, but it was your strategy that brought Damien to justice. Without your detective's intuition, he would have gotten away with murder," Jeez stated plainly.

"That was then; this is now," Tom summarized.

"Sounds like a lot of denial."

"Denial?"

"You need to think for yourself. Listen to what people tell you and evaluate it. Don't accept advice at face value.

"Hmm."

"BTW. Mary Magdalene has been asking about you for these past six years," Jeez concluded.

Tom straightened up. "You mean Leo?" He said pretending not to remember her insistence on being called Mary Magdalene, not Leo.

"Yes. Of course," Jeez responded. "Let's hear

what she has to say about your contribution."

Jeez helped Tom stand up and handed him the reins to a horse.

"She is still in Nazareth?" Tom inquired.

"Yes, but we have to hurry," Jeez responded. "We are all off to Caesarea Philippi this evening."

"We?" Tom said looking astonished.

"We," Jeez responded.

∞

Tom watched Jeez mount his horse, then followed suit. As they then trotted down the trail towards Nazareth, Tom's mind was flooded with vivid memories of their adventures together with Leo six years prior:

- How Damien and his crew rode down that same trail with Mary Magdalene bound and gagged on a donkey and had threatened Jeez with a sword;
- How Marcellus had commissioned him and Jeez as auxiliaries outside of Megiddo and assigned them the task of freeing Mary Magdalene from human

traffickers;

- How Jeez had healed the slave trader's son and rescued Mary Magdalene;

- How Marcellus had been attacked by a scorpion as they slept that night in Nazareth, and how Marcellus sent the three of them—Jeez, him, and Mary Magdalene—to pursue Damien to Sebastian;

- How Marcellus had given Mary Magdalene the *nom de guerre* of Leo;

- How a band of brigands had attacked Leo.

- How Damien and his crew were brought to justice by Tribune Claudius on the road to Jerusalem.

Most importantly, Tom remembered his father's passing and the oath he had made at the funeral, *gladius* in hand, to follow his father to become a police officer. *Why had his vow that at twelve seemed so right, so vivid, gradually faded into the ethers in the years that followed?*

Jeez turned to look at him and smiled. It was as if he read Tom's thoughts and said, "It will come back to you." The stress simply drained from Tom's face.

Chapter Three

*A*s they entered Nazareth in late afternoon, news of their arrival spread quickly. Mary Magdalene rushed out to meet them. As Tom dismounted, she threw her arms around him. Jeez dismounted and ran over to greet his mother, Mary, who he called Emah.

"I'm sorry that I'm late," Jeez said.

Emah greeted him with open arms and shared what was on her heart, almost like a prayer. "You're just in time for the first *Shavuot* meal, featuring milk-related menus. The barley harvest was plentiful this year. We've much to be thankful for, not just the giving of the law on Mount Sinai to Moses, but especially for your safe arrival home."

Jeez presented Tom with Mary Magdalene still wrapped around him. "Mother, you remember my friend, Tom."

"Yes. Of course. Welcome," Emah responded, smiling more than a bit.

"Before we sit down to eat, let me take care of the horses," Jeez requested.

"No. No. No. I will take care of the horses," Mary Magdalene volunteered. She took the reins of the horses and walked them around to the small stable behind the house.

Emah ushered Jeez and Tom to the table under the awning in front of the house. There they removed their helmets, armor, and *gladii*, and sat down. Emah quickly returned with a jug of wine and some dates. After a few minutes, Emah and Mary Magdalene returned with food. Jeez offered a blessing, and they all sat down to eat.

"Where is the rest of the family?" Jeez asked.

"They all traveled with relatives and the Nazareth community to Jerusalem for *Shavuot* celebrations," Emah reported.

"Now, I feel guilty that you stayed behind just to celebrate *Shavuot* with me," Jeez responded. "Thank you."

"It is the least that we could do. After all, your salary keeps us fed, clothed, and sheltered," Emah assured him.

"It is my privilege to serve you," Jeez said, looking Emah eye to eye.

"Why are you late? Why is Tom here?" Mary Magdalene asked.

"With Tom's help, I must travel to Caesarea Philippi this evening," Jeez answered.

"Caesarea Philippi? Couriers between here and there routinely disappear or are murdered," Mary Magdalene blurted out, giving Jeez a stern look. "Caesarea Philippi has a sketchy background."

"Sketchy in what way?" Tom asked.

Mary Magdalene looked at Jeez.

"It is within walking distance of the ancient city of Dan, one of the lost tribes of Israel that was symbolized as a snake, remained associated with idolatry, and relocated from their covenantal land near Joppa. Later, when King Jeroboam broke away from Israel, he erected a golden calf at Dan," Jeez continued.

"Wasn't Samson from the tribe of Dan?" Tom asked.

"You really know your scripture. Dan relocated from tribal lands near Joppa. Samson's family stayed behind, which is why he later became beguiled of Philistine women," Jeez remarked.

Jeez glanced at Emah. "Keep in mind that we don't

need to hang out with these people, just deliver a message," Jeez said.

"Sound like we will need to travel at night and take an escort," Tom responded.

Mary Magdalene crossed her arms and looked at Jeez. "Have you been to Caesarea Philippi before?"

"No. But the route is obvious. The road to Caesarea Philippi simply follows the Jordan River north of the Sea of Galilee through the Hula Valley to its source at Mount Hermon," Jeez responded without hesitation.

"Yes. That is the direct route, but the entire Hula Valley is plagued by lions, brigands, and disease-carrying mosquitoes. My late father always traveled east of the Sea of Galilee through the Tetrarchy of Philip to Nawa, up the King's Highway, and across the Golan Heights to Caesarea Philippi," Mary Magdalene said.

"That's not direct," Jeez observes.

"Perhaps, but the Roman roads are more heavily traveled and mostly free of bandits. It adds four hours to the trip on horseback, making an eight-hour trip more like twelve," Mary Magdalene replied. "Is your assignment time sensitive?"

"No timeframe was specified," Jeez responded, "but I'm likely to get lost if I travel unfamiliar roads without a guide."

"I can guide you. Will Marcellus lend me a horse and a uniform again?"

"Actually, I anticipated this issue and brought everything you need," Jeez said.

"Great," Leo said, pinning up her hair, "we need to get started."

∞

"Whoa! Listening to you two talk about the challenges of this journey is a bit overwhelming," Tom remarked smiling.

"So, my role here is to provide a military escort through a foreign country?" Tom asked. "I'm not sure that I'm up to chasing off lions and brigands in the middle of the night.

"There is strength in numbers, and you're definitely the courageous one in our little circle," Leo said gently.

"The last time we went on an adventure, we had the

backing of Tribune Claudius and his men. This time we will be on our own," Tom responded.

"King Antipas assigned me this mission, which implies that in theory Tribune Claudius still has our backs," Jeez stated.

So, we will be carrying a message from King Antipas to his brother, King Philip?" Tom deduced. "In other words, we will be disposable players in an Herodian intrigue?"

"Now that you mention it. Yes. That describes our prospective situation," Jeez observed.

"Now, you have me interested. There is nothing worse than being disposable and being stuck on the sidelincs," Tom summarized.

"As I said, you're the courageous one around here," Leo said with a smile. "We should be on our way."

"Right," Jeez said.

"Okay then," Tom replied.

∞

At twilight, Leo donned her uniform and Emah filled gourds with water for the trip. Jeez, Tom, and Leo mounted their horses and left on the road to Cana. There, they followed a wadi trail to the southern tip of the Sea of Galilee. Night-time travel along the eastern shore of the Galilee was lit up by a full moon that illuminated not only the sea, but also fishing boats on the water.

They followed the trail along the shore of the Sea of Galilee through Hippos in the Decapolis, past the heights at Gergesa. Then, they crossed the border into the Tetrarchy of Phillip. No one stopped to question them or break the silence of a night ride. This even as they passed bonfires lit by night watchmen, whose job it was to collect taxes on the border.

"Why has no one stopped us?" Tom inquired. "Are these borders unpatrolled at night?"

"The border guards are looking for smugglers hauling fish or other valuables on donkey carts, not auxiliaries riding horses," Leo explained.

When they reached the Roman road east of Nawa, they picked up the pace.

∞

At Nawa, they stopped to water the horses before taking the road to Damascus. There they ran into a Parthian caravan, whose leader complained about the heavy taxes at each stop along the route.

Tom stopped to talk with one of the traders. "Why are you traveling along the King's highway?"

"We transport eastern spices, like pepper, cumin, and dill, and Persian carpets for sale in Alexandria where we purchase wine, dates, and olives for the trip back to Susa," the trader explained.

"What about the conflict between Rome and Parthia?" Tom inquired.

"At the moment everyone seems civil, though there is a lot of intrigue over Armenia and Mesopotamia," the trader opined.

"So, the borders are still in play?" Tom asked.

"Always," the trader summarized before wandering off.

∞

Leo signaled that it was time to go. Tom and Jeez mounted their horses and together with Leo they set off north on the road to Damascus. Soon, they reached the cut-off to the Golan Heights, and the pace slowed as the road to

Caesarea Philippi took them uphill. As the morning light appeared over the horizon, they saw Mount Hermon covered in clouds off in the distance.

As Leo led Tom and Jeez downhill from the Golan Heights into Caesarea Philippi, they passed in front of the Grotto of Pan, a large cave at the base of Mount Hermon.

"See that spring? It is one of the headwaters of the Jordan River. People say that it is too deep to be plumbed. The Romans call it the Gates of Hell." Jeez observed.

They rode past a temple next to it, with several statues standing in rock window-sills carved into the face of the cliff, overshadowing the Grotto, and came to Philip the Tetrarch's palace just west of the Grotto.

"What is that temple?" Tom asked innocently.

"It is the Roman Temple of Pan," Jeez explained. "Philip renamed the city of Panias to honor Caesar Augustus (and himself) and made it his capital."

"Who was Pan?" Tom asked.

"Pan was a Greek god with the head and torso of a man, and the body of a goat usually pictured playing a Syrinx (or panpipes)," Leo interjected. "The Romans practiced bestiality—sexual relations with animals—in the Temple."

"Sorry I asked," Tom said

"You have heard the expression, old goat, which describes a lascivious old man? Guess where it comes from," Leo continued.

"What? That is an abomination to the creation mandate of God. Human beings are to rule over the animals, not degrade themselves with them," Jeez said stone faced with a whisper.

"How can a Jewish ruler tolerate such a blatant violation of God's law?" Tom complained.

Tom and Jeez stopped their horses and just stared speechless at one another.

"Aren't we just delivering a message?" Leo piped up.

After a few moments, they rode over to the entrance to Philip the Tetrarch's palace and dismounted. Jeez presented the palace guards with the message written out by Antipas for his brother Philip. An auxiliary took charge of their horses, and a tribune led Jeez, Tom, and Leo into the palace.

∞

While Tom waited with Jeez and Leo outside

the throne room in Phillip's palace, his mind began to wander. He remembers a conversation that he had with his mother when they discussed his college plans.

"Where would you like to attend college, and what do you hope to study?" his mother asked.

"Several local schools have solid criminal justice programs," Tom began. "Studying locally will save us money and allow me to see Micha on weekends."

"Your test scores suggest that you could study just about anything, anywhere," his mother observed.

"I know what I want to study," Tom replied.

"Your grandparents have encouraged you to prepare for medical school, especially at an Ivy-League college. They promised to pay expenses," his mother continued.

"I feel guilty accepting their money."

"The rumors that they earned their fortune selling illicit drugs are simply not true."

"Then why do they still dress like flower children from San Francisco?" Tom asked.

"That's not fair," his mother objected. "They

have supported us, ever since your father died."

"Not fair because they supported us, or not fair because they made their fortune selling drugs?" Tom asked.

Upset, Tom's mother walked out of the room. At that point, Leo tapped Tom on the shoulder, and his mind returned to Philip's palace.

Chapter Four

*T*he tribune ushered Jeez, Tom, and Leo into the throne room. Philip the Tetrarch sat on his throne with Antipas' manuscript in front of him. Next to his throne was a statue with the head and torso of a man with the body of a horse.

Philip read the manuscript out loud. "Greetings. I trust that you're well and have recovered from your trip to Rome. How are Herod and Herodias? What word do you have from them?" Philip looked up to Jeez. "Did my brother communicate anything further?"

"Only his sincere concern for your health and his wish to see you once again," Jeez said ad libitum.

Philip smiled. "From his youth, my brother was an accomplished liar."

"You know him better than I," Jeez observed.

"Tell him that our brother and his wife are in good health. Caesar Tiberius has requested Antipas come for formal consultations in Rome as soon as is practical. Herod would also enjoy a social visit. Herodias kept asking about Mary Magdalene, who had been her companion from Sepphoris," Philip recounted.

"Very good," Jeez responded. "Your majesty, may I ask you a question?"

"Go ahead," Philip replied.

"What is the significance of the statue next to your throne?" Jeez asked.

"That is a figure of Chiron, the son of Apollo. He is the wisest of the Centaurs and mentor to the greatest of warriors. He teaches them medicine, herbs, music, archery, hunting, gymnastics, and prophecy," Philip explained.

"Thank you for the explanation," Jeez said.

"Judging from the time of your arrival, you must be hungry and tired. The tribune will take you to our kitchen and show you to the barracks where you can get some sleep. This afternoon you'll have a manuscript to carry back to Sepphoris to Antipas," Philip indicated.

"You're most kind," Jeez observed.

In the kitchen, an attendant helped them clean up and offered them a bench at a table to sit. The cook then brought a pitcher of wine, goat's milk cheese, flat bread, figs, and grilled mutton. As they sat and ate, a centurion from the Sebastian cohort came and sat next to them.

"You were wise to travel at night east from Sepphoris, instead of north along the Jordan River, to reach this place," Dante observed.

"How do you know all that?" Tom asked.

"Villagers in the Huleh valley around the Jordan River are unhappy with Philip's rule." Dante recounted. "They express their discontent by hanging his couriers in a tree, believing that they will be cursed by God."

"How do you know all that?" Tom asked.

"Patience. Patience. I was instructed by my tribune to follow you and make sure that you arrive in Caesarea Philippi safely," Dante replied.

"That is an odd request coming from a tribune

of the Sebastian cohort," Tom noted.

"Odd indeed. He never acts without consulting Herodias, even when she is in Rome," Dante said.

"Why would she take an interest in us?"

"No idea, but she must be your guardian angel," Dante opined and excused himself, retreating to the barracks.

Jeez, Tom, and Leo finished their meal and followed Dante to the barracks to sleep.

∞

Late in the afternoon, the tribune woke Jeez and handed him a scroll.

"Your horses have been groomed and fed. You can leave for Sepphoris whenever you're ready," the tribune explained.

"Thank you, sir," Jeez replied.

Jeez woke Tom and Leo. They cleaned up, ate, and departed by way of the Golan Heights just before sunset on Saturday evening. At the top of the ridge, Tom looked back at Caesarea Philippi and saw Dante following them at a distance.

∞

As they traveled across the Golan Heights, the images of Chiron and the Grotto of Pan stuck in Tom's mind. He thought: *How could a Jewish leader so blatantly violate God's law of creation, committing such blasphemy with the enthusiasm of religion?*

Jeez too looked troubled and prayed repeatedly out loud through the night: "Lord, why have you brought me to this time and place?"

They traveled seemingly ignorant of the passage of time and space as night wore on. When the sun came up, they rode into Sepphoris.

Chapter Five

*I*n Sepphoris, Jeez, Tom, and Leo dismounted in front of Antipas' palace and asked the guards for permission to see the King. Tribune Claudius came out and, seeing Jeez, waived them into the throne room where they removed their helmets. Antipas appeared surprised to see them. Jeez handed Claudius Philip's scroll, who took it, walked up to the King, and handed it to him. Antipas opened the scroll and read it, then motioned for Jeez to approach the throne.

"Caesar Tiberius has summoned me to Rome for political talks. Did Philip have any comments about this summons?" Antipas inquired.

"No. Nothing beyond the usual pleasantries and an invitation to stay with your brother and his wife," Jeez answered.

"How convenient. A trip to Rome could take months. What would our father think; what would he do? Philip or Herodias' minions could seize Galilee or Perea while I am gone," Antipas speculated.

"No ruler in the region is strong enough to keep the roads clear of bandits, let alone claim new territory," Jeez observed. "Besides, Tiberius would not be happy to hear of strife among his client states."

"Astute observation," Antipas conceded. "My father's ghost roams the halls, but Tiberius still rules the palace."

"One thing that has bothered me—A centurion from the Sebastian cohort tailed us to and from Caesarea Philippi, ostensibly to assure our safe passage," Jeez related.

"Dante?" Antipas asked.

"Yes," Jeez answered.

"He is harmless. However, Dante serves Herodias with more devotion than most," Antipas said. "Herodias has expressed interest in your sister, Mary Magdalene. Do you know why?"

"I only know that Mary Magdalene spent time years ago at the Sebastian court as Herodias' companion," Jeez said.

"Yes. Mary Magdalene served as my ear in that

court," Antipas looked away distraught.

"My brother Herod was never enough for Herodias and he drowned his sorrows in wine, wild parties, and other women. Herodias must grow weary and lonely in Rome," Antipas confessed. "If we must appear before Tiberius, then you must send for your sister to join us on the trip."

"I will see to it," Jeez responded. "May I have a day to retrieve her and prepare my mother for our absence?"

"Of course," Antipas replied. "Today is Sunday. Have her join us on Tuesday, ready to depart."

"Thank you, your majesty," Jeez said.

Jeez backed away from the throne, turned and left the room followed by Tom and Leo. They then put on their helmets, retrieved their horses, and rode to Nazareth.

∞

When Jeez, Tom, and Leo arrived in Nazareth, the entire village turned out to see them, although many had not yet returned from *Shavuot* celebrations in Jerusalem. Jeez shared with Emah their plans to travel to Rome with King Antipas on Tuesday. Emah could see that they were exhausted. Even though it was just shy of noon, Emah helped them clean up, fed them, and helped them retire to an inner room.

Jeez, Tom, and Leo woke after sunset to find that the village had erected a large bonfire in front of the house. The fire lit up the entire community. A slaughtered lamb was basting on a spit in front of the fire.

"Come, tell us the story of your trip to Caesarea Philippi and your meeting with the two Herodian Kings," Emah insisted.

"There is not much to tell," Jeez responded. "King Antipas sent us to King Phillip to inquire about his brother's trip to Rome. Now, King Antipas has been summoned to Rome by Caesar Tiberius himself, and we've been ordered to accompany him."

"What? No fights with bandits or wild animals?" Emah asked.

"No. No. No. We traveled at night to avoid bandits while everyone slept and stayed clear of lion country by traveling through the highlands," Leo explained.

"No fights with bandits or wild animals, but we passed a temple of Roman abominations at the headwaters of the Jordan River," Jeez recounted. "We must thank God for his hedge of protection and guidance from the many temptations during the trip just concluded and the one yet to come."

A feral cat got all the scraps of mutton she wanted and purred herself to sleep. The village idiot danced around the fire waiving his hands this way and that. The local busybody listened intently and imagined all the rumors she could start and pass around in the morning.

The call for stories finally came to an end. Grilled lamb and wine were passed around until the bonfire burned out and the embers cooled in the evening air. No one went home hungry, and everyone slept well through the night.

ACT TWO

Chapter Six

Monday morning, the travelers slept late. Mid-morning, they arose, washed themselves, and breakfasted on dates and goat-milk cheese with flatbread. Mary Magdalene packed up her uniform, brushed her hair, and cleaned her robes to look presentable as a young woman.

Around noon, pilgrims returning from Jerusalem recounted a story of a workplace accident where the tower of Siloam collapsed, killing eighteen workers. Hearing the account, Emah became anxious about Jeez traveling to Rome.

"What will I do if you're shipwrecked at sea or killed in a far-away land?" Emah implored.

"We are all under God's care, no matter what we do or where we travel. There is safety in numbers, and we will enjoy the protection of King Antipas," Jeez assured her.

"Don't you have that backwards? As an auxiliary, you're responsible for the King's protection, not the other way around," Emah responded.

"Safety in numbers means everyone is safer," Jeez reminded her.

Emah appeared at peace hearing Jeez's statement.

∞

Tom groomed the horses, hanging out behind the house. Mary Magdalene noticed that he was missing and went out to look for him.

"Do you think the horses have been rubbed down enough?" Mary Magdalene teased.

"Brushing the horses helps me relax," Tom answered. "I should be studying right now, not chasing around."

"Studying? What do you study?" She asked.

"I'm preparing to study medicine and become a doctor," Tom replied.

"I never met a doctor. You must be rich because only Romans have money for physicians," Mary Magdalene said.

"Not at all. My grandparents support my studies," Tom replied.

"I'm sure you're capable of just about anything, but what does your father do?" Mary Magdalene asked.

"My father was an auxiliary, a police officer, who was recently killed on the job," Tom explained.

"I'm sorry," Mary Magdalene touched Tom's arm.

"Thank you. I apologize for burdening you with my problems," Tom said.

"Don't worry about it. Thank you for trusting me with your grief," Mary Magdalene concluded.

Jeez came looking for them. "We should head out. Who knows what preparations we need to help with in Sepphoris?"

"You're right, let's go," Mary Magdalene confirmed.

They all packed their horses. Jeez and Mary Magdalene said goodbye to Mary. Tom thanked Mary for her hospitality. Then, they mounted their horses and set off for Sepphoris. A neighborhood dog ran playfully alongside of them as they left Nazareth.

∞

When Jeez, Tom, and Mary Magdalene arrived in Sepphoris mid-afternoon, they reported immediately to Antipas' palace, where they found Marcellus in charge of a skeleton crew.

"Why is there a light guard today at the palace?" Jeez inquired of Marcellus.

"King Antipas and his entourage left two hours ago by ox cart for Caesarea Maritima by way of Megiddo," Marcellus reported. "Tribune Claudius left word for you to catch up with them there."

"I was told that we would leave for Rome on Tuesday," Jeez replied. "Why the change in plans?"

The tribune noticed that Centurion Dante followed you to Nazareth and felt it was safer to leave early and avoid being observed," Marcellus explained.

"Smart move," Jeez noted. "How come I was told that Dante was harmless?"

"No idea," Marcellus commented. "Dante is as crafty as his matriarch, Herodias. No one trusts him."

"Thanks for the insight," Jeez responded.

Jeez turned to Tom and Mary Magdalene. "Let's go water the horses at the barracks. It is at least half a day's ride to Caesarea Maritima."

∞

At the barracks, Jeez said to Mary Magdalene. "We've a dangerous ride ahead of us this afternoon. It might be wise to resurrect Leo. Tom and I will water the horses while you get changed."

"Good idea," Mary Magdalene replied, unpacking her uniform, helmet, and *gladius*."

Meanwhile, Jeez retrieved three *hasta*s and shields from the armory.

"Fond memories of the Jezreel Valley?" Tom joked.

"Nothing like a lion attack to get you to skip lunch and put a death grip on your *hasta*," Jeez replied.

Horses watered, the three heavily armed auxiliaries set off down Sepphoris hill on the road to Megiddo with a donkey in tow, packing their belongings.

∞

On reaching the hill overlooking the Jezreel Valley towards Megiddo in the distance, Tom pointed at the entourage close to the river halfway to Megiddo.

"King Antipas' ox cart and security detail are approaching the river, ignoring a gaggle of buzzards circling just ahead of them."

"No. No. No. What is wrong with them?" Leo belted out.

"This cannot be good," Jeez remarked.

"Let's ride," Tom shouted, spurring his horse forward.

The three auxiliaries sped at a canter towards the riverbed. As they drew closer, they heard shouting and it became clear that four lions were ravaging the entourage. Antipas' security detail fled bloodied towards Megiddo, leaving Tribute Claudius alone with *gladius* in hand to defend the King's cart against the lion pride.

Tom shouted as he charged at the lions, driving his *hasta* deep into the side of one lion. His horse reared, dropping him to the ground. Standing up with his shield in one hand and his *gladius* in the other, he attacked a second lion head-on. Still mounted, Claudius attacked a third lion. The remaining lion ran off, leaving three dead lions as the King witnessed the entire spectacle.

Leo retrieved Tom's horse. As she handed him the reins, King Antipas spoke: "I have never witnessed such gallantry in the face of certain death. Who is this auxiliary?"

Jeez responded: "This is my friend Tom."

"From now on, this is Centurion Tom," Antipas declared.

Tom looked at Leo and smiled. "Thank you, your majesty."

Claudius dismounted, walked over, and shook Tom's hand. "Thank you for saving my life," Looking around, back and forth, he said: "Hmm. We should leave this place."

Everyone nodded in agreement, and they proceeded on to Megiddo. On the way, the security detail joined them with reinforcements, including city archers. No one said anything seeing the bloodied gear on Tom and Claudius, but three auxiliaries returned to the riverbank to gather trophies from the lion carcasses.

∞

In Megiddo, Claudias presented Tom with a helmet featuring a silver Crista Transversa, the mark of a centurion, and an ornate bronze breast plate to replace the standard armor worn by auxiliaries. "Centurion Tom, it is an honor to have fought alongside of you. Your courage displayed today shows that you're a leader among men to be emulated by all."

The entourage remained at the garrison in Megiddo to rest, water the horses, and enjoy a cooked meal.

∞

Mid-afternoon they set off for Caesarea Maritima, traveling south of Mount Carmel, being careful to avoid the border with Syria and to remain in Judaea. A couple hours into the journey a rider from the Megiddo garrison rode in at a gallop and reported to Tribune Claudius.

The rider saluted. "Sir, three of the auxiliaries from your cohort were ambushed at the riverbank. The auxiliaries were killed with the sword, stripped, and left in the open for the wild animals."

Claudius returned the salute and asked: "Who did this?"

'The perpetrators were not identified, but the audacity of the crime suggests someone more powerful than typical brigands who normally avoid soldiers," the rider opined.

"Are you suggesting a military force?" Claudius asked.

"A military force cannot be ruled out," the rider replied. "An inquiry is being made, but nothing further has been reported."

Claudius dismissed the rider, who turned and rode off towards Megiddo.

∞

Claudius instructed the driver to stop the King's

cart. "Several security team members were ambushed, returning to the riverbed in the Jezreel Valley, which suggests that we are being followed. It is not clear who is involved, but they may be close behind us."

"What does this mean?" King Antipas asked.

"We need to know what threat we are facing," Claudius responded. "Let me post an auxiliary to drop back quietly and observe to see if we are being followed."

"Very good," the king responded. "Post our new centurion."

"My thoughts exactly, your majesty," Claudius replied.

∞

At the foot of the hills, the road passed through a *wadi* and entered a forest half a mile away.

Claudius turned to Tom. "Wait here at the edge of the forest and watch to see if anyone is following us. Then, report back immediately on numbers and disposition."

"How long should I wait before catching up?"

Tom asked.

"No more than two hours, as we will soon reach Caesarea Maritima," Claudius responded.

Tom saluted and hid himself and his horse behind a thicket in view of the road and the *wadi*. He stuck his *hasta* in the ground in the sunlight and marked its shadow. Jeez and Leo rode on with Claudius and the entourage.

Tom watched the road for about half an hour when he saw Centurion Dante come down the hill on a horse alone. Seeing no one else, he picked up his *hasta*, mounted his horse, and galloped to catch up with the entourage. Reaching the group, he rode up beside Tribune Claudius.

Tom saluted. Claudius returned his salute, pulling disturbed Tom out of earshot of the group. "Sir, only one man, Centurion Dante, is following us."

"What's the problem?" Claudius asked.

"If I wanted to plan an ambush and knew the destination, I would wait near the destination and send someone to keep tabs on them in case their plans changed," Tom responded.

"I see your point," Claudius responded. "Caesarea Maritime is the largest walled city in Judaea. One could easily hide an army there and just wait for our arrival at the eastern gate, where this road enters the city."

"What if we entered another gate?" Tom asked.

"Hmm. We could enter the northern gate by the aqueduct, or the southern gate by the palace, without being expected or seen, if we were careful," Claudius said, stroking his beard.

"What if we sent the cart to the eastern gate as a diversion and took King Antipas to the southern gate by horseback?" Tom suggested.

"I like that idea. I will send the security detail with the cart to avoid any suspicion while I ride with the Fiercesome Threesome and the King to the southern gate," Claudius directed.

"Fiercesome Threesome?" Tom asked.

"That's the nickname given to you and your friends in Judaea after Damien and his crew disappeared six years ago," Claudius explained.

"You and your men dispatched Damien and his crew," Tom responded.

"Yes, but the Judaeans never figured that out, and the myth of the Fiercesome Threesome made for better storytelling," Claudius stated with a wry smile.

"Good to know," Tom said.

Chapter Seven

*T*ribune Claudius directed one of the auxiliaries to trade places with King Antipas—horse, armor, helmet, gladius, and *hasta*. Dressed, Antipas looked like any other auxiliary, only better fed and with fewer scars than most.

Claudius tells the diversion team: Enter the city after dark; Proceed to the Promontory Palace in the morning.

Tom watched the cart roll off. "Does the security team understand the risk inherent in entering the city?"

"They must have known the moment the King traded places with the auxiliary," Leo replied.

"They know the risk. Everywhere outside of Galilee, the King is vulnerable. The Herodians aren't known for their hospitality, and the allegiance of the new Roman Prefect in Judaea, Valerius Gratus, is weighed in shekels," Claudius stated out of earshot of the king. "The Prefect seldom wanders far from Promontory Palace in Caesarea Maritima by the Mediterra-nean Sea."

"Why is that?" Tom asked.

"The Prefect is said to be a middle-aged swim-mer who spends his afternoons in the palace pool," Claudius responded. With the cart out of sight, Clau-dius led them off the road a mile further south.

Riding along, Antipas turned to ask Jeez. "Hero-dias specifically asked that Mary Magdalene join us in Rome. How come I haven't seen her?"

"I'm sure that she'll join us at the palace," Jeez responded, smiling at Leo.

∞

Approaching the wall of Caesarea Maritima af-ter dark, the five travelers found the gate closed. Illu-minated by torches on the wall above him, Claudius shouted to the guards above: "Inform Prefect Valerius Gratus that a messenger from King Antipas of Galilee has arrived and requests that the gate be opened."

"How can that be? The King's cart was attacked a mile from west gate by bandits, and his entire entourage were killed and torched," responded the guard.

Tom leaned over to Claudius and whispered: "How does the guard know whose cart was attacked after dark?"

"The King remains safe. The cart and security team were a decoy," Claudius shouted to the guard. "I'm the tribune of the Sepphoris Cohort with a message from the King to the Prefect."

"I'll inform the Prefect," the guard replied.

Claudius exchanged glances with Tom and whispered, "We are riding into the lion's den. Be aware of your surroundings and say nothing."

After almost an hour delay while the Prefect finished a leisurely dinner, the guard returned and opened the gate.

∞

The guard accompanied Claudius and his team to the entrance of Promontory Palace. Dim torchlight barely illuminated and the sound of pounding waves overwhelmed their footsteps as the palace guard walked Claudius and the others up the marble steps to the threshold of the Prefect's throne room on the second floor of the palace.

Claudius removed his helmet. Valerius Gratus called him into his throne room by name. Confidently, Claudius entered the room. The others removed their helmets and shuffled in behind him like lost sheep.

"Claudius, old friend, how long has it been since we've seen each other?" Valerius said with obvious familiarity.

"Six years ago, we served together in the Teutoburg Forest when the Germanic tribes ravaged three entire Roman legions. Tiberius recently sent his son, Germanicus, with a force to avenge our losses there," Claudius recited.

"So, you do remember," Valerius said with a wry smile. "I refrain from reciting that story as it does not normally engender much glory or honor."

"You fought well in those battles, which Tiberius confirmed and honored in sending you to Judaea, if I recall correctly," Claudius said.

"If I fought well, you fought better," Valerius

pointed out. "After all, you were among the youngest soldiers to earn the rank of tribune, not related to family standing."

"You're most gracious," Claudius responded.

Valerius' demeanor changes. "The guard mentioned that you had a message for me."

"I have a favor to ask. King Antipas has tasked me to travel to Rome with a message for his brother, Herod. Can you recommend a speedy ship traveling that way?" Claudius said, looking at Antipas.

"There is a first-class ship traveling tomorrow morning via Alexandria. Here, let me write a letter of introduction for you to her captain," Valerius said.

"You're most generous," Claudius responded.

"There will be five of you?" Valerius asked.

"Yes," Claudius replied. "If there is room for all of us."

"Actually, yes. This ship regularly brings my carrier pigeons to Rome and travels nearly empty in the off-season," Valerius explained.

"I forgot that you're a stickler for communication," Claudius observed.

"Hmm. I did not know that my procedures were so widely known," Valerius grumbled out loud.

"*Timely news carries the market like timely instructions carry the battle* is a proverb that you used to recite," Claudius said, quoting Valerius' own words.

"You have a good memory," Valerius said, handing Claudius a scroll to read, roll up, and seal.

"I had a good teacher," Claudius said, buttering Valerius' bread.

"Off with you," Valerius said. "The morning comes early for corveta captains. The winds blow westerly off the mountains in the dead of the night, so they are preparing to leave even now."

Valerius instructed a guard to lead Claudius and the others to the ship straight away.

Chapter Eight

At midnight Valerius' guard led them to a cor-veta-style ship roughly sixty feet long with two sails that was docked in the harbor. The guard approached Captain Euphron and handed him a scroll with Valerius' introductions.

The captain looked up from the scroll at Claudius and said: "The Prefect has paid your fare to Ostia from his own account, but we've no provision for your horses."

"I can buy your horses for the Caesarea Maritima Cohort," the guard responded, handing Tribune Claudius seven gold *aurei*. "You can redeem your horses on your return."

"Thank you, you're most generous," Claudius responded, as the guard departed.

"I'm Captain Euphron," he motioned with his hand towards the gangplank. "Find a spot on the deck to be comfortable. When the westerlies pick up, we will shove off," Euphron declared.

"When is that?" Claudius asked.

"Usually around the third hour," Euphron replied.

"What about food and water for the trip?" Claudius asked.

"You can share in our supplies," Euphron explained, "the menu is limited to items that pack well—hardtack, salted beef, dried fish, lentils, beans, cheese, olives, dates, and lemons—but my wife is a good cook."

"How long is the trip?" Claudius persisted.

"Weather permitting, we should reach Ostia in three weeks," Euphron responded.

Claudius and his team boarded the ship and settled in near the bow. Because of the long day and the late hour, they all fell asleep in minutes.

∞

Tom woke up Wednesday morning with the sun in his eyes and the ship well on its way. The westerlies had subsided, and the captain was exploiting the offshore breezes generated by the morning sun to maintain a steady pace up the Judaean coast.

Eager for conversation, Euphron asked him: "Is this your first time at sea?"

"No. My father was raised in a seagoing family and used to take us sailing on the bay in the summertime," Tom replied. "How long have you been at sea?"

"All my life," Euphron responded. "My first memory was of my excitement running to the Ostia docks to welcome my father back from a trip."

"Where is Ostia?"

"Ostia is a port on west coast of Italia near Rome."

"So, you're Roman by birth?" Tom asked.

"No. My father grew up in Corinth and moved to Ostia after serving in the Roman army for many years, but not long enough to earn citizenship."

A seagull flew past the mast.

Euphran continued, "he met my mother when he was stationed in Carthago. He bought this ship with money he inherited from his parents."

"So, you're well-traveled and likely speak many languages," Tom observed. "How long before we reach

Alexandria?"

"We should pass the halfway mark late this afternoon near Gaza. Alexandria will take another day's journey, if the fair weather holds up and we keep up the current pace," Euphron explained.

"You're worried about the weather?" Tom asked.

"Always," Euphron explained. "If the offshore breezes remain favorable, we can continue up the Afri coast as far as Carthago before jumping across the Mediterranean, avoiding the prevailing west-to-east trade winds. That would put us on the Italia coast, cutting the length of our journey.

"And if the winds aren't favorable?" Tom asked.

"If not, we will need to make the jump and work our way up the far coasts of Anatolia and Graecia, which is much harder. One way or the other, the weather determines the timing and path of our journey."

"Sounds complicated," Tom commented. "What is the name of your ship?"

"I call her Luxia which means light because she is patient, meticulous, determined and works at her own pace with a mind of her own," Euphron explained.

Luxia passed Gaza on schedule. They stopped at Alexandria for two days to take on supplies. They left Friday morning. Winds were favorable, and the ship made its way to Carthago, where the captain jumped off. They crossed the Mediterranean sailing west of Sicily.

∞

One day into the three-day trip from Carthago to Ostia, a cold, westerly wind came up over the Mediterranean in the night as they passed north of Sicily. Clouds formed overhead, lightning crashed, and wind-driven waves began to toss the Luxia and sent waves crashing over her decks.

The captain struck the sails and set a storm anchor off the stern, but the ship continued to flounder.

Holding onto the deck railing for dear life, Tom noticed that Jeez slept undisturbed and woke him. "Don't you care whether we live or die?"

"We won't die. Have faith." Jeez replied. "This too shall pass."

"Forgive me, Lord," A wave crashed over Tom and the rolling deck. "Do something!"

As lightning flashed, the entire crew and all the passengers saw Jeez stand up on the deck. With his hands raised and without losing his balance in spite of howling wind and water cascading across the deck, he calmly said, "Be silent."

The wind ceased; the waves subsided; the clouds dissipated; the night gave way to the twilight of dawn.

Everyone stared at Jeez but remained silent. Jeez sat down again, leaned against the railing, and fell asleep as if nothing had happened. The captain and crew returned to their duties.

Antipas turned to Claudius. "Who is this auxiliary that the wind and waves obey him? He silenced both Zeus and Poseidon. Even Hades does not contend with him."

Leo listened to this conversation but said nothing. The Greek gods of the sky, sea, and dark underworld seemed strange to her, and wondered why Antipas did not use their Latin names.

∞

Exhausted and drenched with seawater, Tom's mind began to wander back to when his father took him duck hunting on a flat boat along an inlet on the Chesapeake Bay. Taking his first shot, he capsized the boat, dropped the shotgun in the water, and clung to the overturned boat with his father beside him.

"Dad, I'm sorry," Tom apologized.

"We can buy a new shotgun. I'm just glad you're okay," his father replied.

"I'm not sure that duck-hunting is my thing," Tom responded.

"Let's sort that out later," his father suggested. "The question today is what you learned from this experience."

"Next time I shoot, I will wait until my target is off the stern or bow of the boat," Tom replied, "so the discharge won't destabilize the boat."

"Good thinking," his father responded. "I screwed up by positioning the boat broadside to the birds. This accident was my fault, not yours."

"A bigger boat might also have helped," Tom said with a smile. "What do I do about the duck that I shot?"

"Let's retrieve it and call it a day," his father said. "No reason to go into details when we tell your mother."

The morning sunlight soothed and warmed Tom as he dozed off on the waters just off Ostia in the second week of June.

ACT THREE

Chapter Nine

As the Luxia drew near to the docks at Ostia in late morning, Antipas leaned over the railing next to Claudius, admiring the Roman naval ships anchored off the shoreline beaches. The mouth of the Tiber River could be seen in the distance, along with river barges being loaded with stores of seagoing vessels for the twenty-five-mile trip upriver to Rome.

"Tiberius served as *quaestor* of Ostia before becoming Caesar and built the first forum in the city to strengthen the grain and salt trade, milling, and transshipment of supplies to Rome. My brother, Herod, now holds that position, which is why he has become fantastically wealthy and built homes in both cities," Antipas recounted.

"That means that we will have no trouble finding him, and he will be able to help us prepare for your audience with Tiberius," Claudius speculated.

"Indeed. I only hope that Herodias won't be too disappointed that Mary Magdalene did not accompany us on this trip," Antipas remarked.

"Perhaps, Mary Magdalene will turn up on her own," Claudius assured him, giving Jeez the eye.

"Little chance of that," Antipas responded.

∞

Having overheard the conversation between Antipas and Claudius, Jeez turned to Leo and whispered: "Maybe now is a good time to have Mary Magdalene make an appearance."

"Let's wait until Antipas is comfortable resuming his own persona. Giving up my disguise may draw attention to Antipas' own charade and pose a threat to his life."

"Good point," Jeez responded. "We don't know what traps and temptations lie ahead."

"Herodias is a dangerous woman who may view Antipas as a threat to her husband. Who knows what assassins lie in wait at the Ostia docks?" Leo opines.

"Good grief," Tom exclaimed, overhearing this conversation. "Is there really so much intrigue in this place?"

"Didn't you used to say: Just because you're paranoid, doesn't mean they aren't out to get you," Jeez said, quoting Tom back at him.

"That was just an expression," Tom replied.

"It's not an expression; it's an insight," Leo commented.

∞

Immediately upon docking at Ostia, a delegation of soldiers came aboard to retrieve the carrier pigeon cargo and official mail. Crew members then went through the manifest, noting what cargo needed to be delivered and to whom.

As Claudius and his team prepared to disembark at Ostia, Claudius asked Euphron: "Are you returning to Caesarea Maritima?"

"Yes. Because of our governmental patrons, we are on a regular schedule traveling to and from the Levant," Euphron responded.

"When do you plan to leave?" Claudius asked.

"We will be here a week. If you're interested in returning to Caesarea, let me know sometime soon."

"How do I find you?" Claudius asked.

"You can find us here at the docks during the day, or in our apartment at night. Look for the tall building two blocks from the Ostia forum," Euphron responded.

∞

Claudius and his team disembarked around noon and walked to the Ostia forum carrying their belongings. There, Claudius entered the *curie* where he approached the consular tribune.

"Can you direct me to Herod, prince of Judaea?" Claudius asked.

"Tiberius called him to Rome earlier this week to address the flood on the Tiber River after the recent *medicane*," the tribune explained.

"When will he return?"

"You might inquire at his palace, a block east of the forum. His wife, Herodias, should be able to tell you more," the tribune said.

Leo glanced at Tom and Jeez with apprehension.

"Could you direct us to this palace?" Claudius

asked.

"My attendant will take you there," the tribune pointed to an auxiliary standing by.

"You're most helpful, thank you," Claudius responded.

The auxiliary led them to the palace.

"Is there a tavern where we might get some hot food and a bath before presenting ourselves to the princess?" Claudius asked.

The auxiliary pointed to a nearby building. "Try that tavern. It offers excellent hot food, heated baths, and live entertainment."

Tom winked at Leo.

Claudius thanked the auxiliary and gave him a denarius. "Wait two hours. Then return and announce our arrival to the princess before coming to retrieve us."

"As you wish," the auxiliary responded with a salute.

∞

At the tavern in early afternoon, everyone ate a

meal consisting of grilled swordfish, fresh wheat bread, wine, and olives. While they enjoyed their lunch, a young Mauri woman danced, clapped, and sang as her Roman husband played the lute.

Afterwards, Leo excused herself to wash her hands and change into a robe while the men bathed themselves in a heated pool. Before the men returned, she managed to charm the tavern steward out of a vial of his wife's perfume. As the men put their uniforms back on, Antipas added an expensive hooded robe over top of the uniform, which together gave him a hint of nobility.

When they got together again, Jeez turned to Antipas, who now presented himself as King Antipas of Galilee, and said, "This is my sister, Mary Magdalene, who arrived last week by another ship and stayed with friends."

Mary Magdalene bowed before the king, who alone seemed oblivious to her alter ego and never inquired about Leo's disappearance.

"I'm so pleased to see you," Antipas said warmly.

The auxiliary returned to escort the group for the short walk to the palace. At the palace, the auxiliary presented the group to the tribune leading the palace guard, saluted, and returned to the *curie*.

∞

The tribune inquired of Herodias whether to admit King Antipas, Mary Magdalene, and his guard. Herodias returned with the tribune to welcome her guests. She wore a white silk toga over a purple *stolla* with gold earrings that each dangled two pearls which clicked together as she walked. Her hair style, an *orbis comarum*, featured a high fringe of curled hair at the front and a wreath of braids at the back of the head.

"Antipas, I see that you brought Mary Magdalene. How nice of you," Herodias said with obvious interest in him. "You have just missed your brother. Tiberius summoned his trusted protégé to Rome this morning to help with flood relief."

"When do you expect him to return?" Antipas inquired.

"Who can say? You must follow him to Rome," Herodias instructed. "My tribune will provide horses and accompany you," she said placing her hand intimately on the tribune's shoulder to his obvious discomfort. "Leave Mary Magdalene with us here—we've so much to catch up on."

Smiling uncomfortably, Mary Magdalene exchanged a quick glance at Tom, standing next to her.

"Very good," Antipas responded. "How soon can we leave?"

"The horses can be brought around in a few minutes. The trip along the Via Ostiensis can take an hour or two. You should be at our palace in Rome in time for a late dinner," Herodias explained, gesturing with her hand east towards Rome. "Our palace is on the left off of the Via Ostiensis inside the Servian wall at the western foot of the Aventine Hill, close to our market warehouses."

"Sounds like a good location for an avid merchant," Antipas observed.

"Exactly. I married a first-class peddler," Herodias summarized, only half joking.

Mary Magdalene elbowed Tom without a word or glance.

The horses quickly appeared, and Antipas disappeared just as quickly with the tribune and his guard, leaving Mary Magdalene alone with Herodias, a light guard, and her attendants.

Chapter Ten

With Herodias' tribune in the lead and the sunset at their back, Antipas' trip to Herod's palace in Rome unfolded precisely as Herodias described. On arrival, the tribune introduced Antipas as Herod's brother, and the servants care for the horses. Herod's tribune led Antipas into the house where Herod met his brother in the atrium.

"*Shalom*, brother," Herod said to Antipas throwing his arms around him. "So good to see you again."

Claudius, Jeez, and Tom followed Antipas into the atrium, which had a pool fed by rainwater from a sloping open-air roof. Mosaic tile covered the floors around the pool with menorahs in each corner and each quadrant depicted a different scene from the Hebrew scriptures: The Akedah, the crossing of the Red Sea, the giving of the law, and the dedication of the temple.

"I really like your palace here. I see that you haven't forgotten your heritage," Antipas told Herod.

"Rome is open to Jewish customs, but cringes at the idea that there is only one god, YHWH, and has a taste for pork," Herod said.

"Worshiply idling idols and greedily porking pork?" Antipas asked.

"Ha. It may take you a while to get used to Rome," Herod summarized.

"Can I ask a question?"

"Of course," Herod responded.

"My ship, the Luxia, sails in a week," Antipas stated. "Is that enough time to meet Tiberius' desire for consultation?"

"I meet with Tiberius at the palace in the morning. You can ask him yourself," Herod replied.

"Very good," Antipas said.

A servant walked in and whispered in Herod's ear. "Dinner is ready. I hope that you're hungry. Here in Rome, we take dinner very seriously."

∞

In Ostia, Mary Magdalene dined alone with Herodias. Herodias picks at her food and savors a large glass of wine, which a servant girl quickly refills.

"What is your impression of Antipas?" Herodias asked.

"He is above my station. I do not know him personally, having lived in Nazareth, not Sepphoris, these past six years," Mary Magdalene answered.

"Since your adopted father, Augustine, was murdered?" Herodias callously mentioned.

"Yes." Mary Magdalene turned away from Herodias.

"But you must know his reputation and some of the people around him, such as Claudius," Herodias posited.

"King Antipas is known as an honest man without obvious vices. People like him. Likewise, Claudius came to Sepphoris as one of the empire's youngest and most talented tribunes," Mary Magdalene offered.

"Why does Antipas travel with such a small security team?" Herodias asked.

"Half of his security team was ambushed and killed outside of Caesarea Maritima," Mary Magdalene shared.

"Who was behind this attack? Why did the attack fail?" Herodias chugs her glass of wine contemptuously.

"We traveled separately, so I never heard the whole story," Mary Magdalene responded, continuing the ruse started earlier with Antipas.

Mary Magdalene asked for a tour of the palace after dinner. She feigned ignorance of political matters and talked excitedly of men and Roman fashions, hoping that Herodias would lose interest in her and stop asking about Antipas.

Chapter Eleven

*H*erod's household was up two hours before sunrise, preparing for the day. Claudius cleaned himself up, retrieved some breakfast in the kitchen, and sought Herod's tribune for advice.

"Tell me about security in Rome. Should my men carry shields and *hastas*, or just *gladii* in protecting Antipas?" Claudius asked the tribune.

"Rome has its share of bandits, criminal gangs, and political assassins, who can show up on a moment's notice from alleys off of each boulevard. Herod expects a guard of at least six auxiliaries," the tribune explained. "Even Herod carries a gladius when we walk the streets."

"Six auxiliaries? That sounds excessive," Claudius remarked.

"Julius Caesar was assassinated years ago in the Curia of Pompey here in Rome, northwest of Capitoline Hill. Sixty men were implicated in the attack," the tribune recounted. "The attackers sought to restore the

Roman Republic, but Julius Caesar's assassination led to the reign of Rome's first emperor, Caesar Augustus, who formalized Rome's empire."

"Over sixty assassins? I had no idea," Claudius observed. "In Galilee, most ambushes take place along the roads in the country, and those bandits typically avoid detachments of two or three auxiliaries."

"You're fortunate. Rome is the largest city in the known world with more than one million inhabitants. Tiberius himself has suggested establishing an urban cohort to police Rome's streets," the tribune recounted, "but it still has not happened because no one wants to pay for it."

"Sounds like a good idea," Claudius commented.

"My advice, because there are only three of you, is to carry whatever arms you have, because we travel on foot in the city," the tribune recommended.

"Thanks for the warning."

∞

One hour before sunrise, Herod directed his

tribune to assemble his security detail. Antipas asked Claudius to lead the march with Tom and Jeez. This way Antipas could walk with Herod for the couple blocks down the Via Ostiensis past Palatine Hill and left on the Via Sacra through the forum to the entrance to the Domus Tiberiana, the palace where Tiberius lived. The plan was to visit with Tiberius while he ate his breakfast at a seat in the atrium before he began day's official duties.

At the door to the atrium, Herod stepped forward to confer with the steward attending Tiberius. As he approached the door, he was rudely pushed aside by a detachment of the Praetorian Guards who hurried past Herod and the steward, and spoke a Germanic dialect as they entered the atrium.

Tom turned to Claudius and asked: "Why do these guards speak a Germanic dialect?"

"Since Caesar Augustus, the Praetorian Guards have been recruited from the German provinces so that their loyalties would be exclusively to Caesar," Claudius responded.

"These men aren't guards; they are assassins," Jeez interjected. "They spoke openly of killing Tiberius in German as they entered the atrium."

"How do you know that?" Claudius asked.

"I speak their language," Jeez replied.

A shout went up from inside the atrium. Hearing this, Tom burst through the door, startling and pushing aside the guards inside to see a Praetorian Prefect raise his *gladius,* standing in front of Tiberius' seat. He threw his *hasta* at the Prefect, running him through. He then ran up to Tiberius, tossed his shield to him, and turned with *gladius* in hand to confront the other guards.

Seeing their leader dead, the mutinous guards ran off, leaving Tom standing with Tiberius and the dead Prefect. After a few moments, Tiberius' loyal guards arrived and gave chase to the mutineers, leaving Tiberius standing with Tom's shield.

The room was deathly quiet.

Silently, the steward directed servants to clear out the Prefect's corpse. Hands shaking, Tom sheathed his *gladius,* Tiberius handed Tom his shield, and the steward cleaned and returned Tom's *hasta*. Tom sat on the floor. Unperturbed by Tom's presence, Tiberius returned to his seat.

∞

The danger having passed, Tiberius motioned to Herod to approach his throne and whispered "Who is this courageous centurion?"

"I don't know. He just arrived with my brother, Antipas, from Galilee, as you requested."

"It may be time to hear from Antipas," Tiberius stated, still whispering.

"This centurion is Tom," Antipas replied.

"You mean Tribune Tom," Tiberius responded, motioning to the steward. "Bring my sword."

The steward returned with a ceremonial sword in a golden sheath. Tiberius asked Tom to approach his throne and kneel. He took the sword, unsheathed it, tapped Tom on either shoulder, and then re-sheathed the sword.

"Arise, Tribune Tom," Tiberius said. "I'm forever in your debt." He then handed the sword to Tom.

Motioning again to the steward. "Offer Tom some breakfast and dress him as a proper tribune while I visit with King Antipas of Galilee."

Antipas steps forward to confer with Tiberius. The steward leads Tom, who was still shaking, to the kitchen.

In the kitchen, the steward fitted Tom with soft leather shoes, a silver helmet and breastplate, and a cloak with a purple stripe around the edges consistent with his new status as tribune to wear over his armor. Afterwards, he serves Tom breakfast.

∞

Tom returned to join Jeez in standing guard with Claudius. Seeing Tom's new clothes, Claudius is envious of Tom's new clothing as he wears more functional tribune's attire worn while on duty.

Claudius leaned over to Tom. "Do you know why Tiberius promoted you to tribune?"

"No. Not exactly," Tom replied.

"The Praetorian Prefect, even though an assassin, was also a tribune, whose life is sacrosanct. Only another tribune can kill a tribune without being put to death," Claudius explained.

"What?" Tom exclaimed.

"You may have a lasting problem, however, with the remaining Praetorian Guards, who swore a blood oath to protect their Prefect."

"Good grief. You're telling me that I just got promoted, only to have the meanest gang in the entire empire out to get me?" Tom remarked, looking distressed.

"You ought to know," Claudius exclaimed. "You may want to save your centurion uniform for the trip back home to appear less conspicuous."

Looking at Claudius, Tom replied. "Good advice." After a pause, he turned to Jeez. Thank you for your help. Tiberius is alive because you translated the mutineers' German."

"Law enforcement is your calling, not mine," Jeez replied. "You're my mirror of self-reflection; a catalyst of my empathy. Around you, I feel ashamed of my selfish human nature."

"How can you say that?" Tom responded. "My

recklessness could have gotten us both killed."

"Count your courage as contagious," Jeez observed. "You act on what you know while I avert my eyes. This morning, I noticed the Temple of Saturn and the site where the Flavian Amphitheater, also to be known as the Colosseum, will later be built, financed by the plunder of Jerusalem."

"I have no idea what you're talking about," Tom replied.

"Saturn is the god of agriculture, wealth, and time, which the Greeks called Cronus," Jeez said. "During the Saturnalia festival, Romans spend a week feasting, gift-giving, and fooling around. Hurry-sickness is like Saturn worship, and the temple once served as the Roman treasury."

"So?" Tom commented.

"Walking these streets, I'm haunted by the dead past, present, and future who cry out to me. Children conceived during Saturnalia later exposed to die in the cold by unloving parents; the faithful thrown to wild animals in the Colosseum; the lost roaming the earth without the hope of ever knowing a loving God."

"Oh, my God!" Tom exclaimed.

"How can I live for myself, visited by the voices of the victims, perceiving the pain of those perishing, and haunted by the horrors of history ever before my eyes?" Jeez shared from the heart.

"I'm starting to understand," Tom reflected. "Your finger tips the scales of time more than mine, but we are all called to tip the scales for those who follow."

"It can be a curse to know in the seed, the burning of the tree," Jeez summarized.

∞

As Antipas conferred with Tiberius, Tiberius kept looking at Jeez.

Tom noticed and told Jeez: "Antipas must be repeating the story of your intervention during the medicane the other day."

"My time has not yet come," Jeez stated.

"Such things can't be done in secret," Tom responded.

"I came to save the lost sheep of Israel," Jeez

protested. "Rome is more interested in money and power. How can they reach a deep understanding of God without a compass to guide them?"

"You're asking the wrong guy," Tom replied. "Our relationship has always been personal, not theological. How can I offer you advice on such things?"

"Still, you speak truth to me in your supposed ignorance."

"A taste of heaven may motivate smart people like Tiberius to begin a spiritual journey, digging deeper into what they do not understand," Tom hypothesized.

"They need a spiritual guide," Jeez summarized. "Signs and miracles have to be explained. They require interpretation."

"Interpretation? You mean, as when on the Luxia Antipas explained the storm's sudden calm in terms of the Roman pantheon—Zeus, Poseidon, and Hades—despite his upbringing in Judaea?" Tom inquired.

"Exactly," Jeez exclaimed. "Who would see a Messiah in action without knowing the scriptures?"

"Maybe it is enough for now that the Romans know where and how God may be sought," Tom suggested. "A fuller revelation can come later."

"You're smarter than you look!" Jeez giving Tom a wink.

∞

Antipas asked Tiberius: "How long do you need me for consultations?"

"Why do you ask?" Tiberius responded.

"Most of my security team was ambushed and killed even before I left Judaea. Even here, I have only minimal protection. I fear that Galilee is not secure as long as I'm away." Antipas replied.

"Granted," Tiberius exclaimed. "But who has designs on your kingdom? I'm concerned that my border territories in the Levant are too weak to serve as an effective buffer with Parthia."

"Parthia has never posed a threat. The threat to Galilee arises with more local greed and jealousy," Antipas explained.

"Hmm," Tiberius observed. "It seems that your

father's strength has debilitated his own children. What happen if Parthia wakes from its slumber and marches toward the Mediterranean?"

"Rome would need to intervene. The states in the Levant can barely keep the roads clear of bandits, let alone stand against Parthia," Antipas summarized.

"Your observations reinforce comments that I have heard from others. You realize, of course, that I must bolster my presence in Judaea and Syria to address this weakness," Tiberius stated.

"Galilee would benefit from such a move, as Parthia would have no incentive to break the peace," Antipas responded.

"Our talks have been helpful. You may return to Galilee at your earliest convenience," Tiberius said.

"Thank you, we share a kindred spirit. I apologize for our weakness and the costs that it imposes," Antipas concluded as he backed away from the throne. "Please let me know if I can be of any further assistance." Reaching the door, Antipas led Herod and the security team out.

Chapter Twelve

*I*n late morning, Antipas and Herod walked back to Herod's palace with their security details through Rome's busy streets.

"You realize that under less enlightened leadership, Syria would just absorb Galilee," Herod told Antipas.

"Sure, but Rome's only interest in Galilee is the fish trade, which has more likely caught the eye of our brother, Philip."

"Not true. Philip makes good money collecting taxes on the road to Damascus and on his wine and olive trade," Herod responded. "And he just adores his younger brother, Antipas—at least more than his older brother, Herod!"

"I never understood his antipathy towards you," Antipas stated.

"Philip was always ambitious, always competitive," Herod responded. "However, his antipathy disappeared after our dear father murdered our brothers,

Antipater, Alexander, and Aristobulus."

"You may have it right. It is claimed that Caesar Augustus joked that, It is better to be Herod's pig (*hus*) than his son (*huios*)," Antipas said.

"I figure that Philip's attitude started to mellow after he began to view me—being older—as his life insurance," Heros said.

"You could be right," Antipas paused. "How is it that you came to marry our beautiful cousin, Herodias? She is more ambitious than even her father, Aristobulus, and is twice as dangerous."

"At one point, she enjoyed our frequent trips to Rome," Herod answered. "But, what do you do when your wife stops laughing at your jokes?"

"You're asking your single, younger brother for advice about women?" Antipas asked rhetorically.

"Sorry. I'm fresh out of older brothers to ask," Herod responded with a bittersweet smile. "Perhaps, I should consult a *Mithraic Pater* or Sibylline Oracle."

∞

As the Antipas and Herod procession traversed

Palatine Hill on Via Ostiensis, a large cloud of dark black smoke appeared in front of them. Anxious, Antipas urged everyone to double time down the road. Before they could see what was burning, a thunderstorm erupted, and a heavy downpour of rain fell on them. The rain was so heavy that they are blinded, and the entire group took shelter under a large tree. When the storm cleared, they walked to Herod's palace, which lay in smoldering ruins. Only the stable was spared, where Herod found the servants gathered.

"What happened here?" Herod asked the steward."

A mob with torches swarmed the palace and set it on fire, under the direction of a hooded man dressed as a Praetorian Guard," the steward explained.

"You're sure of this?" Herod inquired.

"The man tried hard to conceal his identity, but I recognized him," the steward responded.

"Are the horses alright?" Herod asked.

"Yes. All of them," the steward answered.

Herod turned to Antipas. "Take the horses you

need and leave for Ostia. I need to return to the *Domus Tiberiana.*"

"Can I help?" Antipas asked.

"No. You may be the one targeted here, not me. Return home to Galilee immediately," Herod responded. "I have friends at court that I can rely on, but you do not."

Antipas hugged his brother. "Be safe." Herod directed the servants to ready the horses. Antipas and his team mounted and left.

∞

After so much talk about Roman fashions, Herodias took Mary Magdalene to a *tabernae,* a Roman tailor shop, featuring a terracotta sign out front picturing an elegantly dressed woman with stylish hair. Inside was a statue of the Roman god, Janus, associated with beginnings, transitions, and endings, depicted with two faces.

The rectangular room displayed tunics, cloaks, and fabrics of hemp, linen, wool, and silk hanging on the walls. In the back was a cutting table and a small room for trying on the clothing offered. Most fabric was its natural color, but some were bleached white and even sported purple stripes for those with aristocratic taste.

Mary Magdalene walked in, gasped, and twirled, cupping her hands over her mouth in total amazement. "What is all this?"

"This is the premier woman's shop in Ostia," Herodias replied.

"Oh goodness," Mary Magdalene exclaimed. "Back home in Galilee, we make all our own clothes. We have fabric shops, but no clothing stores."

"Most Roman women also make their own clothes," Herodias responded. "Only the wealthiest women patronize this shop to look for custom cloaks, tunics, and *stollas*."

"I can see why," Mary Magdalene observed.

"Across the street, one can buy the most exquisite cosmetics and get one's hair styled," Herodias added.

"Oh, my," Mary Magdalene exclaimed.

At this point, a Praetorian Guard in a hooded cloak entered the shop, walked up to Herodias, whispered in her ear, turned, and walked out.

"Who was that?" Mary Magdalene asked.

"Herod sent a messenger. Antipas and his security team will arrive shortly," Herodias said with a smile.

"Will I finally get to meet Herod?" Mary Magdalene inquired.

"No. Herod remained in Rome," Herodias said.

Herodias motioned towards the shop entrance, walked past the statue, and led Mary Magdalene back to the palace.

∞

When Antipas and his security detail got out of sight of the City of Rome, he stopped and changed into his auxiliary uniform. Tom donned his centurion uniform, and gave his tribune uniform to Claudius, keeping only Tiberius' sword. When they reached Ostia, it looked like Tribune Claudius traveling with his security detail.

Antipas addressed Claudius: "Drop us off at the tavern and retrieve Mary Magdalene. Tell Herodias that I went ahead with my security detail to make arrangements for the voyage back to Caesarea Maritima."

"Good idea. Who knows what treachery lurks for us here in Ostia?" Claudius opined.

In front of the tavern, Antipas, Tom, and Jeez dismounted and gave Claudius the reins of their horses, who then rode with the horses to the palace.

∞

When Claudius showed up at the palace with the horses, Herodias was livid. "Where is Antipas?"

Claudius tried to tell her, but she raged in all directions, bouncing off the walls and screaming. In her excited state, Herodias ranted and raved, making threats, and conjuring all manner of evil, past and future, real and imaginary. When Herodias disappeared upstairs, Mary Magdalene gathered her things and left with Claudius.

Passing through the front door, Mary Magdalene and Claudius found several servants crouching on the porch. Even as they reached the tavern, screams and breaking glass could be heard behind them at the palace. Claudius asked: "Why was Herodias so angry?"

"Herodias prides herself on being a dancer. While you were in Rome, she practiced a dance routine for hours to honor King Antipas. She even hired a troupe of musicians to accompany the routine. She does not handle disappointment graciously. Even in small things, she throws tantrums like a child. Antipas must be important to her," Mary Magdalene explained.

"Hmm. I see your point," Claudius noted.

When Mary Magdalene and Claudius arrived at the tavern, she suggested that Claudius join the others at the bath and excused herself to change into her uniform. Before the men emerged from the bath, Leo made her appearance. After a leisurely meal, Claudius and his security team headed down to the docks early in the afternoon to find the Luxia.

As Claudius and his team approached the Lux-ia, the crew prepared to sail.

"It is good to see you again," Euphron blurted out. "I thought that we had missed you and would have to suffer another lonely voyage."

"Why are you leaving early in the middle of the afternoon?" Claudius asked.

"We finished loading this morning. A storm brews north and west of us; the harbor is no longer safe.," Euphron replied.

"No longer safe?" Claudius repeated.

"It is safer to be at sea when the wind picks up. We do not want to have the ship smashed against the dock," Euphron stated.

"Good thing that we are prepared to leave," Claudius concluded. "What is the toll for transport to Caesarea Maritma?"

"Valerius Gratus paid your fare," Euphron replied.

"Did he say why he was being so generous?"

Claudius asked.

"He said that you once saved his life in the Teutoburg Forest campaign," Euphron responded.

"Hmm. We fought our way out of that debacle together," Claudius recalled. "My debt to him was no less than his to me after our horses were shot out from under us. We were among the few who walked out alive."

"You two obviously have much to talk about," Euphron observed.

The crew untied the ship and shoved off. With a steady cool wind, they sailed out of the harbor into a choppy sea. Leaning on the ship's stern railing, in the distance Tom spied Herodias and a detachment of soldiers rush into the dock area with horses spooked and dancing around barely under control.

ACT FOUR

Chapters Thirteen

brisk breeze blew the Luxia steadily for two days with little effort down the coast past Antium and Neapolis, and through the Straits of Messana between Italia and Sicilia into the Mediterranean. Favorable westerly winds continued their progress for four days and nights until they found themselves off the coast of Alexandria, the third week in June.

During an evening stop in Alexandria, Antipas treated his security detail to dinner in a tavern ashore.

"How much do you trust your legion buddy, Valerius Gratus?" Antipas asked Claudius.

"Your presence during our last visit was undisclosed and his response to disclosure remains uncertain. Who exactly is the ungodly antagonist pursuing you?"

"Dare I say our hostess in Ostia, Herodias? She alone has ties to the Praetorian Guard and to the bandits that ambushed my cart in Judaea," Antipas observed.

"Your own brother's wife?" Claudius questioned incredulously. "How can a woman hold such grudges and have such influence?"

"Herodias is a woman who perfumes her poison and decorates deceit with smiles that disguise the lurking dangers. I think I am in love," Antipas conceded.

"When she learned that you weren't coming, Herodias threw a fit, screamed threats, and referred to multiple schemes to kill people. Are you certain you can handle such a tempest?" Leo reported.

"That sounds like Herodias. The word is that she does not handle disappointment well and has trouble distinguishing between love and hatred," Antipas observed.

"Herodias' father was an alcoholic and is well-known to have abused all his children, much like Herod the Great. Abused children often grow up with emotional problems," Leo observed.

"Antipas, I'm glad that I didn't grow up in your family," Claudius stated with a smile.

"If you change your mind, I have plenty of other cousins," Antipas responded.

"May I change the subject?" Tom asked.

"What's on your mind?" Antipas inquired.

"The Luxia passes Joppa before it reaches Caesarea Maritima, right?" Tom questioned.

"Yes. Joppa is a two-to-three-hour ride south of Caesarea," Antipas observed.

"Would it be possible to disembark in Joppa, buy horses, and ride past Caesarea Maritima on the Grand Trunk Road before the Luxia docks?" Tom asked.

"There is an active horse market in Joppa. Good horses can trot for three to four hours, long enough to pass Caesarea," Claudius estimated.

"A determined detachment leaving Caesarea could still catch us before we got to Megiddo," Antipas observed.

"Could we convince Euphron to remain in Joppa for a couple of hours?" Leo injected.

"Right. A couple hours lead is all that we would need to escape to Galilee," Claudius added.

Everyone smiled, nodded agreement, and raised their wine glasses in a toast.

∞

Returning to the Luxia, Claudius asked Euphron to plan a stop in Joppa.

"No problem. Joppa's trade has been eclipsed by Caesarea Maritima, despite the natural harbor," Euphron explained. "But you can still get some good deals on Joppa cloth and perfume."

"I thought Joppa was famous for importing cedar from Phoenicia?" Claudius asked.

"That is still the case," Euphron replied. "I don't normally stop there because my government patrons take me to Caesarea."

"Clearly," Claudius replied. "I have friends there that I would like to visit. Is the horse market in Joppa still active?"

"Actually, the black market in horses thrives in Joppa. Traders complain that the market in Caesarea is depressed because the heavy government taxation is unavoidable," Euphron explained.

"How far is Joppa from Alexandria?" Claudius asked.

"We should be there in two or three days," Euphron estimated.

∞

Later Leo cornered Tom, enjoying the breezes on the deck at the bow. "Why did you gift Claudius with your tribune gear? Tribune Tom has a nice ring to it."

"I kept Tiberius' sword. The other gear is incompatible with our mission," Tom explained.

"You're enjoying the mission too much. You're not cut out to be a physician," Leo observed.

"You may be right. I'm too nervous a person to settle for the sedate life of a physician. I suspect that you would make a much better doctor than I," Tom responded.

"Me? No. No. No. I can't stand the sight of blood," Leo questioned.

"Yes, but you're good with people. You listen. You hold your tongue. You give helpful feedback, all things that require too much energy for me," Tom said pointedly. "I only tolerate people. I'm too busy working the angles to listen. I talk too much and never offer feedback on personal matters."

"Really? What do you think you just did? You just praised me, and, then, point by point you demurred about your own talents. How many men can do that?" Leo observed. "You should study law."

"Law? Who me?" Tom objected.

"My point is that you have many talents, but what is God's calling on your life?" Leo asked.

"You don't miss much. I'm not sure what God's calling on my life is," Tom sat on the deck. Leo sat next to him and leaned on his shoulder.

∞

The following evening, as the Luxia passed Gaza, Jeez and Tom found themselves alone on the deck under a starry evening sky. A pair of dolphins raced alongside the ship.

"You haven't said much for most of this voyage. Is there a reason?" Tom said.

"I find myself marking time rather than working to save the lost sheep of Israel," Jeez responded.

"What did Abraham do when he reached the Promised Land in answering God's call?" Tom asked.

"What?" Jeez inquired.

"Abraham traveled the length and breadth of the Promised Land, marking the land with altars to the Lord," Tom said.

"And?" Jeez exclaimed.

"One must survey land before one can develop a strategy to possess it," Tom replied.

"Interesting," Jeez responded.

"What have you learned in your travels?" Tom asked.

"The deprivation of human beings is pervasive. No one is holy or seeks God," Jeez responded. "Even in my own case, I find too much pleasure in the life of an auxiliary."

"Your time as an auxiliary has brought you before high priests, princes, and even the emperor of Rome," Tom observed. "If you had just been a carpenter like your father, your preparation would be incomplete."

"What are you saying?" Jeez asked.

"Your time as an auxiliary not only paid your family's bills after the death of your father, it also contributes to your larger call," Tom pointed out.

"Tom, I appreciate your insights," Jeez declared.

∞

As the dawn broke, the Luxia sailed into Joppa harbor. The captain and crew trimmed the sails and pulled up to the dock. Claudius approached Euphron.

"I want to invite you to breakfast at the Harbor Tavern," Claudius said.

"Thank you, tribune," Euphron replied, "but first let me ask you a question."

"Of course, what is it? Claudius inquired.

"How long do you need me to remain here in Joppa before shoving off?" Euphron asked.

"Why do you ask?" Claudius questioned.

"While we were docked in Ostia, Herodias inquired of Antipas," the captain went on, "but I pleaded ignorance. She seemed to believe me, but she appeared too crafty to pass off lightly. When you asked to be let off in Joppa, I suspected that you, too, were leery of Herodias and her influence."

"Thank you, Euphron. You're a good friend. We need only a couple of hours' head start to ride past Caesarea," Claudius said.

"I have no reason to hurry. I will wait here until this afternoon. We are ahead of schedule; Caesarea won't be expecting us until next week," Euphron explained.

"If anyone asks, we got off at Joppa to travel to Jerusalem to meet Valerius Gratus before the busy fall festivals," Claudius patted Euphron on the shoulder. "Let's go eat some breakfast. After breakfast, we will purchase horses and return to the ship to pick up our things."

Chapter Fourteen

*O*n leaving Joppa, Claudius and his team rode east on the road to Aphek, which joins the Grand Trunk Road along the coast. Before finding the road, Leo asked Claudius: "Can I make a suggestion?"

"What is it?" Claudius responded.

"If I were worried about bandits out of Caesarea Maritima, I would avoid the Grand Trunk Road altogether. "I would travel the road through Lod, then cut across the hill country to the Central Ridge Road through Samaria."

"Hmm. That would avoid ambush along the Grand Trunk Road. Crossing the Jezreel Valley at Jezreel avoids Megiddo," Claudius observed.

"Exactly," Leo opined. "With spies and traitors all about, whom can you really trust?"

"Let's take the road to Lod," Claudius summarized.

∞

Riding through Lod, they ran into a caravan escorting Valerius to Jerusalem, who invited Claudius to ride alongside his cart.

"How was your voyage to Rome?" Valerius asked. "I suspected that I would miss your return."

"Thank you for paying our fare. The voyage was faster than expected, which left time to travel and see the sights in Judaea."

"The sights in Judaea? You're a hopeless romantic. What tourist visits Judaea?" Valerius exclaimed.

"I love a good road trip. My duties usually prevent me from indulging my footloose spirit," Claudius responded.

"I'll bet that you haven't heard the latest gossip from Rome," Valerius teased.

"Gossip? What gossip?" Claudius asked.

"Herodias threw a fit when Antipas left without saying goodbye and later divorced Herod. As we speak, she is traveling by ship to her palace in Sebastian," Valerius reported.

"Really? You got all that from a carrier pigeon message?" Claudius inquired.

"Don't knock carrier pigeons. With the right paper and a skilled scribe, one can write more than most expect," Valerius said.

"What word do you have of Rome?" Claudius asked.

"What do you mean?" Valerius asked. "What are you holding back from me?"

"Mutineers in the Praetorian Guard attempted to assassinate Caesar Tiberius," Claudius reported.

"Are you joking? Is he okay?" Valerius asked. "Who was behind the attempt?"

"Tiberius is fine, but I haven't heard any further details," Claudius said. "I was hoping that you had an update."

"Sorry. This is the first that I have heard about it," Miffed and snippy, Valerius looked away. "Until the next time," he said, pulling back the curtain on his cart.

Claudius and his security detail rode off, taking the road northeast into the hill country to join the Central Ridge Road.

Several hours later, Claudius asked Antipas what Valerius had said. "Do you believe that Herodias divorced Herod?"

"That news is consistent with comments that Herod made when we were talking in Rome," Antipas said. "What do you do when a tempestuous wife loses interest?"

"I never had that problem," Claudius said, "but I remember her wild and uncontrolled rage."

"Yes, but Herodias can also be very persuasive when she wants to be," Antipas remarked without offering details. "The fact that Valerius heard about Herodias' fit of rage suggests that they are in direct correspondence."

"Are you jealous? Are you saying that you would court her attentions when given the opportunity?" Claudius asked.

"Good or bad, there is no woman like Herodias."

Leo looked at Tom with surprise and dismay.

They lunched at the tavern in Shechem and stopped for dinner in Jezreel. At sundown, Jeez, Tom, and Leo asked permission to remain in Nazareth. Claudius and Antipas rode alone back to Sepphoris without incident.

∞

After Claudius and Antipas leave Nazareth, Mary Magdalene shed her Leo persona and asked Tom to go for a walk.

"Are you going to leave me again?" Mary Magdalene asked Tom.

Tom looked at her, taking a long pause. "You remind me of someone."

"Who is that?" She asked.

"Someone that I was once close to, back when I knew who I was, before I started thinking about medicine," Tom responded.

"What happened?" Mary Magdalene asked.

"Life got confusing," Tom responded. "These past few weeks have cleared away the confusion, but you know better than I that I do not really belong here."

"You have always been Tribune Tom. Tiberius

just held up a mirror to you. Have you, like Samson, been beguiled by Philistine women?"

"No. Not really. I just don't want to let my family down," Tom intimated, "especially my grandparents who have supported us since my father died."

"That is admirable, but they need to support you, not only financially, but emotionally." Mary Magdalene explained. "You cannot live out someone else's ambitions, someone else's dreams."

"How do you know all that?" Tom inquired.

"My parents also died, and I have lived with strangers ever since," Mary Magdalene went on. "If I tried to chase after different people's visions of who I should be, I would lose my mind."

"I see your point," Tom confirmed. "Adversity forced you to grow up quickly and to figure out your own calling at a young age."

"You're right," Mary Magdalene confirmed. "So, are you going to leave me again?"

"Yes. Part of who I'm is returning home to those who love me," Tom confirmed, "but let me leave you with something to remember me by."

They walked back to the house, where Tom unpacked his things and handed her Tiberius' sword.

"I can't take your sword," she protested. "It's the mark of a tribune."

"I can't take it with me," Tom explained. "If you must, sell it to support yourself, and Jeez, when you and Jeez figure out your own callings," Tom said.

Mary Magdalene accepted the sword with a quizzical look on her face. At that point, Emah invited them for dinner on the patio.

∞

Jeez and Tom spent the night in Nazareth, but they rose before dawn to clean up, pack their things, and return to Sepphoris.

Climbing the hill to Sepphoris, Tom and Jeez came to the spot where they had first met.

"It's time for me to return home," Tom said, dismounting his horse.

"Of course. Our time has been too short, but answer me this—why did you leave Tiberius' sword with

Mary Magdalene?" Jeez said, also dismounting.

"Don't you know? It is my contribution to your calling to serve the lost sheep of Israel," Tom replied.

"My time has not come," Jeez replied.

"Surely, but I get the impression that you're back on track," Tom interjected. "Your work as an auxiliary is but for a season."

"What are you getting at?" Jeez asked

"This is clearly a lawless time where the law needs to be reinforced. However, enforcing the law is my calling, not yours," Tom said.

"And you're good at it," Jeez said.

"Your calling is to teach people to look beyond the law to love God and all that is good. How can the cycle of sin be broken while the law reminds them of their guilt and sin?" Tom asked.

"A sin offering must be made that captures their attention and grants them forgiveness and freedom from their own guilt and shame," Jeez observed.

"Freedom is good," Tom replied, "but I don't understand the whole sin offering thing."

"Don't worry about it. You have many talents, but you are truly your father's son."

"And so are you. Thank you for helping me sort that out," Tom said.

Jeez ran over and hugged Tom. "Godspeed."

Tom closed his eyes. "Ten, nine, eight, seven …"

Chapter Fifteen

*T*om woke to find himself in his bed in the dorm listening to a white-noise recording of beach sounds. He looked at the clock on his desk that read five o'clock. The South Hall kegger that Cynthia invited him to was still hours off.

The door opened, and Moe came running in.

"What's the rush?" Tom asked.

"The tower club is flying down to Northern Virginia for the weekend. Do you want to tag along?" Moe asked.

"Do I have to jump out of an airplane?" Tom asked.

"No. The flight down to Dulles International Airport (IAD) in a C-130 this evening is gratis, thanks to our Air Force sponsor. The jump tomorrow is a separate flight," Moe responded.

"Count me in. When do we leave?" Tom inquired.

"You've got 15 minutes to pack and be out the

door. The van picks us up out in front of the dorm," Moe replied.

"Roger," Tom responded. "I can pack in five, then I need to text Micha to pick me up at IAD and Larry to watch Climate. Then, we are out of here."

Tom packed, texted, and jumped into the van with Moe. On the trip to Boston Logan International Airport (BOS), Tom texted Cynthia with regrets. By eight o'clock, they had landed at IAD.

"Meet us back at IAD on Sunday at five p.m." Moe instructed.

"IAD on Sunday at five p.m." Tom repeated back, like a soldier on station.

∞

Micha picked Tom up at IAD at eight-thirty Friday evening and drove him to McLean.

"My parents gave me the car with instructions to bring you by the restaurant before taking you home," Micha said.

"This was all very sudden. My mom still doesn't know that I'm in town. What time should I tell her to expect me?" Tom reported.

"Invite her to join us at the restaurant for a late dinner at nine-fifteen," Micha suggested.

"Okay. My mom's a big fan of your father's cooking," Tom responded, as he composed a text to his mom, who immediately responded, accepting the invitation.

"Tell me, why the sudden trip down from school?" Micha asked.

"Nothing special. My roommate flew down with the Tower Club for a parachute jump tomorrow afternoon, and they had an extra seat. I only found out this evening at five," Tom responded.

"Good. Do you want to join the youth group for a museum trip downtown tomorrow morning?" Micha asked.

"Sounds like fun. What's the occasion?" Tom asked.

"There is a visiting exhibit on the Roman Empire and the early church," Micha responded.

"Let's plan on it," Tom said.

"So, tell me about your classes," Micha inquired.

"Funny you should ask. After we texted earlier this week, I decided to broaden my studies. Pre-med is great, but I can meet the requirements and still have another major," Tom explained.

"Oh?" Micha exclaimed. "What major?"

"I have decided to major in criminal justice with pre-med as a minor," Tom went on.

Micha smiled. "That sounds more like the Tom that I know and love."

Tom just looked at her and smiled back.

∞

Saturday morning, Micha picked up Tom at home. They drove to the Metro stop, parked, and took the train into Washington, D.C. getting off at a station stop near the museum.

"What got the youth group interested in this exhibit?" Tom asked.

"There is a sword rumored to have belonged to Caesar Tiberius and to have been passed down through the church in Jerusalem," Micha said.

"That is an odd combination of owners," Tom opined.

"Truly," Micha responded.

When they arrived at the museum, the sword exhibit had a long line of people eager to see it. The youth group got in line and waited. When they arrived at the exhibit and looked in the glass, they saw a large Greek bible opened to and highlighting Revelation 2:16, which in English reads: "Therefore repent. If not, I will come to you soon and war against them with the sword of my mouth." Behind the Bible sat Tiberius' ceremonial sword emblazoned in gold.

When Tom saw the sword, a big smile came across his face, but he said nothing, nothing at all.

ABOUT

*A*uthor Stephen W. Hiemstra lives in Centreville, Virginia with Maryam, his wife of more than forty years. They have three grown children.

Stephen worked as an economist for twenty-seven years in more than five federal agencies, where he published numerous government studies, magazine articles, and book reviews. Check WorldCat.org for a complete listing.

Stephen has published a six-book, Christian spirituality series. He wrote his first book, *A Christian Guide to Spirituality* in 2014. In 2016, he wrote a second book, *Life in Tension*. In 2017, he published a memoir, *Called Along the Way*. In 2019, he published *Simple Faith*. In 2020, he published *Living in Christ*. His sixth book—*Image and Illumination*—was published in 2023.

In 2023, he began his Image of God series with the publication of *Image of God in the Parables* (2023) and *Image of the Holy Spirit and the Church* (2023). *Image of God in the Person of Jesus* (2024) completes this series.

Two books from his Christian spirituality series

are available in Spanish: *Una Guía Cristiana a la Espiritualidad* (2015) and *Vida en Tensión* (2021). Two books from his Image of God series, *Imagen de Dios en las Parábolas* (2025) and *Imagen del Espiritu Santo y la Iglesia* (2025) are also available in Spanish. He also published his first book in German: *Ein Christlicher Leitfaden zur Spiritualität* (2022).

In 2021, he published his debut novella, *Masquerade*, and rewrote it as a screenplay under the title: *Brandishing the Blue*. In 2023, he published a sequel, *The Detour*, and adapted it as a screenplay. In 2024, he published another sequel, *Christmas in Havana*, which has also been adapted as a screenplay that was a semi-finalist in the Kairos Prize[1] competition (2024/25).

In 2025, Stephen began a new series with *Jeez and the Gentile*. *The Reboot* is the second book in this series.

Stephen published his first hardcover book, *Everyday Prayers for Everyday People* (2018). He also published an eBook compilation book, *Spiritual Trilogy*,

---

1 https://www.kairosprize.com/kairos-prize-semi-finalists-2025/

that year.

Stephen has a Masters of Divinity (MDiv, 2013) from Gordon-Conwell Theological Seminary in Charlotte, North Carolina. His doctorate (Ph.D., 1985) is in agricultural economics from Michigan State University. He studied in Puerto Rico and in Germany and speaks Spanish and German.

Correspond with Stephen at T2Pneuma@gmail.com or follow his blog at http://www.T2Pneuma.net.

If you enjoyed *The Reboot*, please post a review online.